THE BASEBALL GEEKS ADVENTURES

Bossing the Bronx Bombers at Yankee Stadium

The Baseball Geeks Adventures Book 4

David Aretha

Yankee Stadium™ is a registered trademark and is owned by The New York Yankees Baseball Club. This story has not been authorized by Yankee Stadium™ or The New York Yankees Baseball Club.

Library of Congress Cataloging-in-Publication Data

Aretha, David.

    Bossing the Bronx Bombers at Yankee Stadium / David Aretha.

       pages cm. — (The Baseball Geeks adventures ; book 4)

       Summary: "When the owner of the New York Yankees invites Joey, Kevin, and Omar to New York to watch a game in the owner's suite, the geeks start finding ways to help the Yankees win. But when people start finding out what's going on, the geeks find themselves running for their lives through the Bronx"—Provided by publisher.

    ISBN 978-1-62285-133-1

    1. New York Yankees (Baseball team)—Juvenile fiction. [1. New York Yankees (Baseball team)—Fiction. 2. Baseball—Fiction. 3. Bronx (New York, N.Y.)—Fiction.] I. Title.

    PZ7.A6845Bo 2014

    [Fic]—dc23   2013029786

Future editions:
Paperback ISBN: 978-1-62285-134-8   Single-User PDF ISBN: 978-1-62285-137-9
EPUB ISBN: 978-1-62285-136-2   Multi-User PDF ISBN: 978-1-62285-170-6

To Our Readers: This is a work of fiction. References in this story are made concerning historical and current baseball players, otherwise any resemblance to actual persons, living or dead, is purely coincidental.

Speeding Star
Box 398, 40 Industrial Road
Berkeley Heights, NJ 07922
USA
www.speedingstar.com

Cover Illustration: © Ingvard the Terrible

CONTENTS

CONTENTS

Chapter 1

THE GEEKS MEET THE GEORGES

So there we were. The Baseball Geeks. Sitting in a luxury suite at Yankee Stadium™. Looking especially geeky in our suits and ties.

"Man, I haven't had to wear a suit since my great-aunt Loretta died in 2010," I complained.

Kevin, our chronically nervous and antsy friend, was rubbing his big front tooth, creating a squeaky noise.

"And I can't take my suit jacket off," Kevin said, "'cause everyone would see my armpit stains. I'm sweating like a pig."

"Yeah, well, I got my own problems," said Omar, our tall, lanky African-Uzbek-American friend. It was obvious that the Big O had outgrown his lime-green suit. "I look like Magic Johnson in Kermit the Frog's Sunday outfit," he complained.

Kevin, Omar, and I were more at home on the Little League fields of suburban Cleveland. But today we were guests of George Robert Rustin Ruffenheimer III, the eccentric, multibillionaire owner of the New York Yankees. GRRR 3, as he was known, was actually a fan of *us*—or at least his grandson was. GRRR 5 had seen us on TV in the "Fenway Challenge," when we prevailed in a treasure hunt inside Boston's Fenway Park.

Now we sat in the owner's suite, an hour before a Yankees–Cleveland Indians game on a Friday night in July. The suite was like the party room of a fancy restaurant, with a bar, tables, and comfy leather chairs. Paintings of Yankee greats, from Babe Ruth to Derek Jeter, lined the walls. Up near the big glass wall, a row of seats faced the field.

While a few millionaire-types milled around, us Geeks sat at a table drinking Sierra Mists. Then the kid walked in.

"Aw, geez, here we go . . . ," said Kevin, who had little patience with youngsters.

GRRR 5 was a plump child, about eight years old—three years younger than us. He wore a wide grin that seemed frozen on his face. Ridiculously, he donned a complete New York Yankees uniform, including a cap and plastic spikes. He stood in the doorway with a woman clad in jewelry—probably his mother. She pointed to us, and the strange boy walked toward our table.

Kevin looked at me and rolled his eyes.

"Be nice," I told him.

The kid walked up to our table and stared at us with that silly grin.

"Hi," he said.

"How's it goin'?" Kevin mustered with a fake smile.

"I'm Joe," I said to the boy, shaking his hand. "And this is Kevin and Omar."

"My name is Georgie," he said. "But most people know me as GRRR."

Georgie turned his face into a snarl and curled his fingers into a claw.

"Grrrrrrrrrrr," he growled.

Kevin and Omar glanced at each other as if to say, *this kid's nuts*.

"I saw you guys on TV," Georgie said. "I watched the 'Fenway Challenge' eleven times."

"Wow, eleven," Kevin said. "You should get a medal."

I kicked Kevin under the table.

"Do you want the lineup?" Georgie asked, placing a piece of paper on the table.

"The what?" Omar asked.

"The manager sends my grandpa the lineup before every game," Georgie said, still with the grin on his face. "My grandpa always wants to see it. My grandpa owns the Yankees."

"Okay, Georgie," the woman shouted from the doorway. Thankfully, the kid had to go.

"I'm your number one fan," he told us.

He turned and walked away. The back of his Yankees jersey said "GRRR" up top and then "5" as his number. We remained composed until the kid left the room, and then burst out laughing. Omar and Kevin each broke into huge Georgie-like grins, each one dumber-looking than the other.

Omar grabbed the lineup card.

"So what's the deal with this?" Omar asked. "Does the owner have to approve the manager's lineup?"

"Don't you know about this guy?" Kevin said. "Ruffenheimer is the most controlling owner in baseball. The manager . . . what's his name?"

"Barney Maxwell," I said.

"Yeah, he's GRRR 3's puppet. His 'yes' man. He gets paid five million dollars a year to take orders from the Boss."

Omar stared at the lineup card. Over the next few minutes, the three of us discussed a pair of bad lineup decisions by Manager Maxwell. Us Geeks may have been just average students, but we *knew* baseball. We especially knew the Cleveland Indians, whom we watched on TV virtually every day.

"I don't understand why Cabellano is not starting," I said. "Against our catcher, he could steal bases all day."

We were lost in our discussion until the Boss cleared his throat. We looked up, where the six-foot-four, large-and-in-charge Yankees owner loomed over us. He wore a blue suit and a cowboy hat with the Yankees' logo on it. Before he bought the team, Ruffenheimer had owned a huge swath of land in Texas. When oil was discovered on his territory, he sold the land for billions. Then he bought the Yankees.

"Howdy, boys," he said, tipping his hat.

We stood up, as if our middle school principal had just entered the room. We attempted to say hello, but the Boss was an intimidating figure. Kevin started sweating like a pig.

"Sit down, sit down!" implored Mr. Ruffenheimer.

We sat down, and he joined us at the table.

"I want to thank you for being nice to my grandson. He's a big fan of yours, which is why I flew you in here."

"Thanks for having us," Omar said.

"I'm curious about what you were talking about there," he said, pointing to the lineup. We tried to say it was nothing important, but he persisted.

"Fess up, boys," he said. "Are you saying we should make a change to the lineup?"

"Oh, no, sir," I said. "We just . . ."

He persisted. "You just what?" he asked.

We went on to suggest that Felix Cabellano, the speedy backup outfielder for the Yankees, should be in the starting lineup. The Indians' catcher had been in a terrible throwing slump lately. "So if Cabellano got on base," Kevin explained, "he could easily steal second and third base every time."

GRRR 3 was intrigued.

"Also," Omar told the Boss, "the Indians' starting pitcher hasn't been getting his breaking ball over the plate against left-handed batters." In his previous two starts, we explained, Cory Fryman had walked nine batters—including eight lefties. "So we think the Yankees should start Justin Rule as the DH tonight," Omar said.

"He's left-handed and really patient," I added. "He would probably draw a couple walks."

"Huh . . . ," Ruffenheimer mused. "He walked eight lefties?"

"Yes, sir," I said.

The Boss held the lineup card in his hand and pondered it for a while. He walked over to the bar, took out a pen, and wrote a couple changes on the card.

"He's not actually changing the manager's—," Omar whispered.

"Shhhhh," I said.

"Ernie?" the Yankees' owner said to a young man in a suit.

"Yes, sir?" Ernie replied.

"Run this down to Barney," GRRR 3 said. "We're gonna make a couple changes today."

"Yes, sir," Ernie said, and he marched out of the room with the card.

The Boss walked back to our table.

"Let's not discuss what just happened here," he warned us. "If the New York media finds out that I got three little rugrats calling the shots, they'll run me out of town! Hahhhh-hah-hah-hah-hah-hah!"

He turned to walk away, but then he stopped to tell us one last thing.

"Oh, and if your changes don't work out tonight," he told us, "I'm firing all three of ya! . . . You'll be *walkin'* back to Cleveland!"

The Boss laughed gruffly, then walked out of the room. Omar, Kevin, and I looked at each other.

"What just happened here?" Omar asked.

"I don't know," I said.

For some reason, my heart was pounding and I had to go to the bathroom—and I'm not talking number one. A bead of sweat rolled down Kevin's forehead, and he started to reek.

"For the first time in my life," Omar said, "I'll be rooting against the Cleveland Indians."

Chapter 2

"How Did We Get Into This Mess?"

It was the bottom of the ninth of a 4–4 game, and Kevin, Omar, and I watched nervously from the owner's suite. While others milled around behind us, we sat in the blue, cushy seats behind the glass that overlooked the field. Kevin, still sweating bullets, munched popcorn like a squirrel. Omar was on his fourth Dr Pepper. I kept score with a pencil, documenting the events that we had helped create.

"Leading off for the Yankees," boomed the announcer through the speakers, "No. 39, Felix Cabellano. The center fielder, Cabellano."

So far, our predictions had come through. Justin Rule, the patient left-handed batter for the Yankees, had drawn *three* walks against the Indians' starting pitcher.

Not only that, but Cabellano—as we had predicted—ran wild on the basepaths, stealing two bases. After the second steal, Mr. Ruffenheimer ran into the suite with three hot dogs for us. "How are my little geniuses!" he beamed.

The Boss left, and now Cabellano led off the bottom of the ninth.

"Just do it, Cabby," Omar muttered.

And he did. Cabellano rifled a shot up the middle for a single, bringing Omar to his feet.

"Yeahhhh!" screamed the Big O. He broke into a lanky-limbed celebration dance.

"Gohhhhh, Cabellano," he sang. "Crack 'em Gangnam style!"

Right then, I got a text from my dad. He and Kevin's and Omar's dads were sitting in a suite near ours. GRRR 3 had paid for all six of us to fly to New York and stay at a nice hotel, but he isolated them in another suite. My dad didn't like that, but you can't say no to the Boss. Anyway, my dad's text said that if the Yankees won in the ninth, the dads would stop by the suite and take us home.

And it looked like they would after Cabellano stole second base.

"Holy crap!" blurted Kevin as he pounded his forehead. "That's his third steal of the night!"

"We are singlehandedly destroying the Cleveland Indians franchise," I said.

The Indians had lost enough games in my lifetime. I couldn't believe I was helping them lose another.

"Do you think if he steals third base," Omar asked, "the Boss will bring us hot cherry pie?"

"I would just tell him," I said, "to make mine à la mode!"

The next batter flew out to left field for the first out of the inning. Cabellano remained at second.

"This would be the perfect time to steal," I said. "A) He would make it, and B) he could then score the winning run on a groundball or outfield fly."

"He's going!" Kevin screamed as he jumped to his feet, his eyes bulging.

The catcher's throw was wide of the bag and in the dirt. Cabellano made it easily. Four stolen bases in one game.

"That ties a Yankees record," we heard someone say.

"This is freakin' crazy," Omar said.

Three pitches later, the Cleveland pitcher uncorked a wild pitch. Cabellano scampered home with the winning run as his Yankees teammates mobbed him at home plate. The crowd went wild, and Frank Sinatra's version of "New York, New York" blared on the loudspeakers—as it does after every Yankees victory.

"I don't believe what we just saw," I said, still in disbelief.

"Wooo-hooo!" boomed the Boss as he ran into the suite. "Let's celebrate, boys! I got ice cream sandwiches!"

He handed one to each of us.

"Why don't you kids come over to my wife's suite? My grandson is there, and we can have a postgame celebration."

I could see in the eyes of Kevin and Omar that they felt like me. We already had our lifetime fill of the Ruffenheimer family. Omar stretched his long arms and faked a big yawn.

"Thank you, sir," he said, "but I think we should probably hit the hay."

"Yeah," I added. "Our dads are on the way over right now."

"Listen," the Boss said, walking up real close to us. "I want you kids to stay an extra night—come back for tomorrow's game."

"Awww, no, we couldn't," Kevin said. "I mean, the expense of the hotel rooms alone . . . it's just too much."

"I own the hotel," the Boss said. "Besides," he said, whispering, "we're under .500. I need your help beating these Indians."

"Yeah," Omar said, "but we gotta get back to school, and . . ."

"*It's July,*" Kevin whispered to Omar out of the corner of his mouth.

"Summer school," Omar said. "We really value the importance of a year-round education."

"I insist," the Boss replied.

"Yeah, but . . . uh . . . ," Kevin mumbled.

"I *insist,*" Ruffenheimer said, this time more firmly.

You couldn't say no to the Boss. We would be back at Yankee Stadium the following day.

As we rode in a limo to the Five Crowns Hotel that night, we explained the whole story to our dads. The reaction was mixed. Mr. Ovozi, Omar's father, was a tall, hardworking electrician from

Uzbekistan. He was a kind man, but he talked in a loud, stern voice with a heavy accent.

"We're supposed to fly home tomorrow!" he bellowed. "I have to work this weekend. I keep hearing about the Boss, the Boss, the Boss. I'm worried about *my* boss!"

My father, a no-nonsense airplane mechanic, didn't like the whole situation. He once served in the National Guard, and he did things by the book.

"What kind of operation do they got running here?" he said. "Let the manager manage the team, and leave our kids alone. When I was your age, the only input I had was filling out the All-Star ballot."

"I think it's still the same way today, Dad," I said. "I don't think every major-league team has three kids making all the decisions."

"I think it's pretty cool," said Kevin's quirky dad as he brushed his curly, golden hair off his round-framed glasses. "The last team I got to manage was my Lebanon baseball team."

Kevin buried his face in shame and shook his head.

"You lived in Lebanon?" Mr. Ovozi asked.

"No, the Lebanon Correctional Facility in Ohio," Mr. Kernacki responded.

Kevin's dad lived a clean life, but many years earlier, he had gone to jail for forgery and burglary. He was still a little bit kooky, which was probably half the reason that Kev was a nervous wreck half the time. Poor Kevin.

As we drove through the Bronx, he looked out the limo window and nervously squeaked his tooth with his finger.

"Well, I read that every game the Yankees win is worth $2 million to the Boss," Mr. Ovozi said.

"Then he should pay us $2 million," Omar reasoned.

"Or at least pay for our dinner tonight," Kevin's dad said.

"Hector," he cried out to the limo driver. "What's the finest restaurant in the Bronx?"

We wound up at Jake's Steakhouse, where Mr. Kernacki went all out, ordering the shell steak au poivre, served with a brandy black peppercorn sauce. "Hey, it's on the Boss!" Mr. Kernacki said. "He told us he'd pay for all our meals."

My dad and Mr. Ovozi wimped out and got pork chops. Omar, Kevin, and I each ordered Jake's Dinner Burger, which was served on an English muffin. None of us kids had much of an appetite, though, and not just because Mr. Ruffenheimer had plied us with hot dogs and ice cream sandwiches. Tomorrow he would expect us to make more ingenious decisions. We were starting to feel the pressure that comes with being part of the New York Yankees.

The pressure intensified the next day when Mr. Ruffenheimer set us up at the conference table in his office. It was just the three of us, as the Boss was out on business. Yet we could feel his presence, largely because a giant painting of him loomed behind his big, fat desk.

His secretary had handed us the lineup card, and Omar, Kevin, and I got down to business.

"It's just our luck that the Indians are starting a rookie knuckleballer, with *two* innings of experience in the majors," Kevin fretted about pitcher Ollie Sickels. "There's no history on him."

"But the key word is *knuckleballer*," I replied. "We need to look up how the Yankees have hit other flutterballers."

The Boss's secretary, a kindly older woman with her hair in a bun, had given us each a laptop, and the three of us went to work.

It turned out that R. A. Dickey was the only other active knuckleball pitcher in the majors, although many Yankees had batted against two former knuckleballers: Tim Wakefield and some guy named Charlie Haeger.

Thanks to Baseball-Reference.com, we were able to calculate the batting averages of each Yankees hitter against these three knuckleball pitchers. Our results were fascinating (well, at least to a baseball geek)!

It turned out that Yankees manager Barney Maxwell put two guys in his lineup, Coco Berry and C. J. Peplowski, who had batting averages in the mid-.100s against those three knuckleball pitchers. But Austin Parker and Aurelio Sanchez, who had ripped .363 and .395 respectively against the knucklers, were on the bench. We were almost giddy with excitement.

"Man, these stats are like . . . gold!" Kevin exclaimed.

"The Boss may get you that cherry pie after all, Omar," I said.

We informed the secretary of our findings, and she said she would call Mr. Ruffenheimer. Minutes later, she escorted us to the owner's suite.

"So what did Mr. Ruffenheimer say?" Omar asked as we walked through the stadium concourse.

"Well . . . ," she replied. "First he said 'yee-hah,' and then he said if you were ten years older, he'd hire you full time."

All three of us broke into grins. I could just picture myself as a Yankees executive, twenty-one years old, making, like, $300,000 a year. I'm not sure what I would do with all that money. Probably buy a new bike and a new mitt, like a Rawlings Primo Italia or a Nike Diamond Elite. Wow . . .

"What would you do," I asked the guys, "if you were making, like, $300,000 a year?"

"I'd buy the world's largest baseball card," Omar said.

He was referring to the ninety-foot-by-sixty-foot card of Detroit Tigers slugger Prince Fielder, which Topps created in 2013.

"Where would you put it?" I asked.

"I'd buy a big mansion with a humungous ballroom," Omar replied, "and I'd lay it out on the floor. Nobody would be allowed in there."

"You're an idiot, Omar," Kevin said.

"Not according to the Boss," Omar retorted.

When we reached the owner's suite, we were surprised to see that no one was there. Even stranger, the big window had been automatically tinted. That meant that no one could see inside.

"What's going on?" Omar asked the secretary.

"Mr. Ruffenheimer would like to keep your involvement with the team hush-hush," she said. "Yesterday you were guests. Today, he wants no one to know you're here. Help yourself to soda and snacks."

And then she left, closing the door.

"Well this is creepy," Kevin said.

Omar went to the bar area and opened the refrigerator.

"Whoa, this fridge is loaded!" he exclaimed. "They got sliced ham, turkey, corned beef . . . like, five different kinds of cheeses. . . ."

Kevin, clearly nervous again, was getting annoyed with the Big O.

"Rye bread," Omar continued his list, "pumpernickel bread, tomatoes, sauerkraut, Thousand Island dressing. Hey, we can make our own Reuben sandwiches!"

Omar put the bread in the toaster, nuked the corned beef, and made himself a Reuben sandwich. As Kev and I settled into the viewing seats, the P.A. announcer belted out the Yankees' lineup. Coco Berry and C. J. Peplowski were out. Austin Parker and Aurelio Sanchez were in—but Manager Maxwell put them in the eighth and ninth spots in the order.

"I bet he put them there on purpose," I said, "because he's mad at the Boss."

"Yeah," Omar said between bites. "He's like: 'All right, I'll play them, but they'll bat where I want 'em to bat.'"

It turned out that Sickels really had his flutterball working that night. He retired the first eight Yankees batters, including Parker, who popped out to shortstop.

"If Parker and Sanchez don't hit," I predicted, "we'll be on the next plane to Cleveland."

"No more Reubens for you, O—," Kevin began to say. But before he could finish his sentence, Sanchez tomahawked a knuckler into right field for a single. Omar stood up and, with his long arms, pretended he was a puppeteer.

"We're da masters of da puppets," he said, adding a little dance move. "Pullin' da strings. Pullin' da strings."

"It's just a crummy single, Big O," Kevin said.

And meaningless, too, as the next hitter grounded out. I got the feeling that of the three of us, Kevin most wanted this managing mayhem to end. Sweat was rolling down his face like an NBA player in overtime.

Through five innings, the game remained a scoreless nail-biter. And then it happened. In the top of the sixth, Parker knocked a Sickels knuckler into the right-field corner for a double.

"If Sanchez drives in Parker with a single," I said, "and the Yankees end up winning 1–0, I swear the Boss will hire us full time."

But Sanchez didn't get a single. Instead, he launched a Sickels knuckler high into the air to right field. The Indians outfielder drifted back, back, back . . . to the warning track . . . to the wall . . ."

"Stay in," Kevin pleaded. "Stay in . . ."

"Gone!" Omar shouted, as the crowd went crazy. Unbelievably, our two guys had singlehandedly put the Yankees up 2–0. Omar broke into a victory dance.

"We're in the money!" he sang. "We're in the money! We're in the money 'cause we're so freaking smart!"

"What money are you talking about?" Kevin scolded. "He's not gonna pay us! We're eleven years old! Haven't you ever heard of child labor laws?"

"They pay child actors, don't they?" Omar replied.

"We're not actors, Omar," Kevin said, slumping into his chair and sighing. "I don't know *what* we are."

Sickels left after the sixth inning, and, sure enough, the Yankees held on to win 2–0. Fittingly, Sanchez ended the game with a beautiful sliding catch in left field. He—*we*—had made forty thousand Yankees fans very happy.

"So what do we do now?" Omar asked.

"Well," Kevin said, "maybe if we just sneak out of here and meet up with our dads, we can hop on the next plane."

"Good idea," I said. "Let me text my old man."

But before I could dial his number, guess who blasted through the door?

"Yeeeeee-hahhh!" squealed GRRR3, running up to us in his Yankees-blue suit and cowboy hat.

Kevin looked like he just saw the sequel to *Nightmare on Elm Street*. Shadowing the Boss was little GRRR5, who again wore his Yankees uniform and that stupid grin on his face.

"You kids are the greatest thing to happen to the Yankees since we bought Babe Ruth's contract in 1920!" Mr. Ruffenheimer exclaimed. His exaggeration and level of excitement were disturbing.

"Y'all need some nicknames. Omar, you're tall and gangly, like Joe DiMaggio, so you're going to be Joltin' Joe."

"All right!" said an honored Omar.

"Kevin, you're a scrappy little guy, like Derek Jeter, so I'm gonna call you Little DJ."

Kevin responded with a forced, uncomfortable grin.

"And Joe?" The Boss said to me. "Hmmm . . . Joltin' Joe is already taken. Georgie, what should we call our friend Joe here?"

"Farty!" Georgie blurted.

I immediately shot a piercing stare of contempt at that little . . .

"No, no, not Farty," the Boss thankfully responded. "Torre, Jr., after our great Yankees manager Joe Torre."

"Boys," GRRR3 added as he led Georgie toward the door, "you're coming back tomorrow, and I'm not taking no for an answer. Arrive at the clubhouse three hours before the game."

He left the room, but not before making one final remark.

"You're our new batboys," he said. "That way, you can make in-game decisions."

As the GRRRs disappeared, Omar's jaw dropped to the floor. Kevin started breathing really heavily—like he was hyperventilating.

"Kevin, it's okay, it's okay," I said, patting him on the back.

He slumped to the floor and tried to catch his breath.

"Joe," he said weakly.

"Yes?" Omar responded.

"Not Joe DiMaggio, you idiot!" Kevin snapped.

"Yes, Kevin?" I said.

"How did we get into this mess?" he asked.

"I don't know," I said. "And I have no idea how to get out of it."

Chapter 3

THREE GEEKY YANKEE BATBOYS

Never in a trillion years would I have imagined this: Omar, Kevin, and me sitting in the corner of the Yankees' dugout, dressed in Yankees pinstripes. We had arrived for the Sunday afternoon game extra early to put on our batboy uniforms and avoid mingling with the players in the clubhouse. But now there was nowhere to hide. The players began to trickle from the clubhouse to the dugout.

"Oh, my gosh—it's Jeter," Kevin said as Derek Jeter entered the dugout and spat on the floor. "I can't let him see my number."

The Boss had made sure that our uniforms included the numbers of the players he named us after. So Omar wore 5 for DiMaggio, I donned 6 for Torre, and Kevin wore 2 for Jeter.

"You got to stand up eventually," I told him. "You're a batboy!"

"Oh, no," Kevin sighed.

Manager Barney Maxwell headed our way carrying the lineup card. He had been a longtime minor-league player and manager. Then both the San Diego Padres and Houston Astros hired him and fired him as their skipper. He took the job as Ruffenheimer's "yes man" because he knew it would be his last chance to manage in the majors.

"So there's the three little know-it-alls," Maxwell said with a grin.

He handed me a lineup card and a pencil. I didn't know what to say.

"All right, fellas," he said. "I'm not crazy about what's been going on here, but Mr. Ruffenheimer signs my check."

He sat down next to us.

"The Boss says you have to make at least one change," Maxwell told us. "And I'm telling you not to make *more* than one. Understand?"

We nodded.

"More importantly," he said firmly, "don't tell *anybody* about this. Got it?"

"Yes, sir," Omar replied.

"Not the players, the coaches, and *certainly* not the media," he said.

"We understand, sir," I said.

"All righty then," he said. "Go to work."

Maxwell left us alone to analyze the lineup. We had already done our homework, and the decision was easy: add part-time slugger Buster Kemp to the Yankees lineup because he had a history of belting slow curveballs into outer space. The Indians' starting pitcher, Randall Crain, threw a lot of slow curves.

I gave the edited lineup card to Maxwell, who added Kemp to the No. 8 spot in the order. We hunkered in the dugout until the bottom of the first inning, when batboy duty finally called.

When the Yankees' leadoff batter popped out, I ran and fetched his bat. I had been on a big-league field before, at Fenway Park, but with forty thousand fans in the stands and major-league stars all around, this was totally different. It was thrilling, really.

Jeter was up next, and Kevin agreed to get his bat. "If he's on the field, he may not notice my number," Kevin reasoned. He was wrong. After Jeter grounded out, the Yankees legend stopped Kev in his tracks.

"Hey, batboy!" Jeter chirped.

Kevin, en route to the dugout with the lumber in his hand, froze like a statue.

"Where did you get my number?" he asked.

"Uhh . . . ," Kevin wavered. "That's . . . just the uniform they gave me."

They entered the dugout together.

"That's cool," Jeter told him. "Where are you from?"

"Cleveland," Kevin said.

"Cleveland!" Jeter said with a grin. "What are you, a spy?"

Several players laughed. Kevin looked very uncomfortable, but Jeter made him feel at ease with a pat on the shoulder.

"Just kidding, kid," he said. "Welcome to the Yankees."

"That was nice of DJ," Omar said.

"Yeah," replied Kevin, who was feeling more relaxed. "He's always been cool."

We settled into our batboy routine, and our nervousness transformed into excitement. At one point, a player asked Omar to run to the clubhouse to get three pieces of bubblegum from his locker. Omar ran the errand, and the guy gave all three pieces to us. I thought that was a really nice gesture.

Buster Kemp struck out in the third inning, but he faced Crain one more time in the fifth. With Crain already approaching a hundred pitches, this undoubtedly would be the last time

Kemp would face him. I wasn't sure what to wish for, so I just sat back and watched. And then the magic happened—again. Crain tried to paint the outside corner with a big curve, but he got too much of the plate. Kemp, a lefty, launched it deep to right.

"You gotta be kidding me!" blurted Kevin as he ran to the dugout steps.

Yankee Stadium erupted as the ball disappeared into the right-field stands, giving New York a 2–1 lead.

Omar, after retrieving the bat, actually high-fived Kemp as he trotted across home plate.

"Every change we've made," Omar told Kev and me as he descended into the dugout, "has been brilliant."

"Shhhh!" Kevin warned Omar. "Keep your mouth shut!"

It was too late. Felix Cabellano, the outfielder whom we had added to the lineup on Friday, shot us a hard glance. He was a very intense guy, and he was instantly curious.

"Hey, No. 5," Cabellano said to Omar. "What do you mean by 'changes'?"

Omar didn't know what to say.

"Uhh . . . nothin'," he mustered. "Nothin.'"

Cabellano stared at each of us suspiciously, then walked to the other side of the dugout.

"What did you have to open your big mouth for?" Kevin said to Omar.

Poor Omar. He felt bad.

"Do you think he's going to squeal on us?" Omar asked.

I looked over at Cabellano, and he simply sat by himself and watched the action on the field. It appeared we were safe . . . until after the game.

The Yankees went on to win 3–1, and afterward we raced through the tunnel to the locker room. The new Yankee Stadium, which had opened in 2009, included an enormous locker room for the home team. Each player got not just a place to hang his clothes, but a stack of wooden cabinets to store stuff. Recessed lights above each locker added to the classy ambience.

We didn't have a locker. We just sat on a couch and frantically pealed off our uniforms while the happy players milled about. But as we pulled our T-shirts and shorts and sneakers out of our duffel bags, Cabellano approached us.

"When you guys are done, I want to talk to you," he said.

I got a funny feeling in my stomach, and Kevin looked nervous again, rubbing his tooth. We got dressed and walked to a quiet corner of the locker room, where Cabellano awaited us.

"Are you guys making changes to the lineup?" he asked.

We just stood there with our mouths open, knowing that either lying or telling the truth would be a very bad idea.

"Come on, guys, spill it," Cabellano insisted.

"You're gonna have to talk to Mr. Maxwell," I said. "We're not supposed to say anything."

"All right," our interrogator said. "Fair enough." And he walked away.

"We've got to get out of this city *now*," Kevin said as we went to grab our duffel bags.

A security guard corralled us and led us toward some doors, and then into the Yankees' private parking lot. Our dads were there to greet us—and did they ever greet us!

"There they are!" Mr. Ovozi blared.

Each of our dads was beaming, and they all wrapped their arms around us. It was strange and uncomfortable.

"What's going on?" I asked.

"We'll tell you in the limo," Kevin's dad said.

As we settled into the limousine and the driver pulled out of the lot, my dad explained why he was unexpectedly joyous.

"Mr. Ruffenheimer . . ." my dad began.

"The Boss!" exclaimed a grinning Mr. Ovozi.

"The Boss met us in our suite after the ninth inning," said my dad as he pulled a check out of his pocket. "He gave us checks for $5,000 each!"

"What?" I blurted.

"And," added Kevin's dad, "he said as long as the winning streak continues, with you guys working your magic, he'll pay us $5,000 per win!"

Omar, Kev, and I were stunned.

"But I don't want to do this anymore," Kevin said meekly.

"Yeah," Omar said. "One of the players was gonna talk to the manager, and—"

"Oh, nonsense!" Omar's dad blurted. "Five thousand dollars a day to be a batboy! It takes me over a month, working nine, ten hours a day, to make $5,000 dollars."

I tried to appeal to my dad—the man of high values, who believed in making money through hard, honest labor.

"This is a great opportunity, Kevin," he told me. "This is money that will send you and your brother to college."

What could I say to that? Nothing. We would just have to suck it up and stick it out.

Back at the hotel, Omar, Kev, and I sulked in our rooms for the rest of the night. The fathers eventually ordered room service—and then groused about the high prices despite the fifteen grand they had pocketed two hours earlier.

The next day, Monday, was an off day for the Yankees, as they waited to start a three-game home series against the Detroit Tigers on Tuesday.

We agreed to Mr. Kernacki's suggestion to go to Coney Island, the famous amusement park in Brooklyn. As if our stomachs weren't already upset—worrying about our Yankee woes—our tummies took a churning at Coney Island.

The spinning teacups started us off on this hot, sunny day, but the scariest ride of all was the Cyclone. This rickety wooden roller coaster had been built in the same year that Babe Ruth belted sixty home runs—1927. I was surprised that Kevin went on it. I'm sure he wished he hadn't. But we survived.

Tuesday was another ordeal. The game wouldn't start until after 7 P.M., so we spent most of the morning and early afternoon in our hotel—waiting, waiting, and waiting.

"Last night," Omar said, "I dreamt that the Yankee players found out about us—and retaliated."

"What did they do?" I asked.

"They took us to the men's room, held us upside down by our ankles, and dunked our heads into the toilets. They just kept on flushing, one swirly after another. It just never ended."

All three of us were noticeably shaking as we entered the Yankees' locker room at 5:30. We looked around at the players. Who knew about us? Anybody? Everybody? It was hard to tell. The players chatted amongst themselves as they prepared for the game. Meanwhile, the three of us sat on the couch and put on our uniforms.

"Hey, Joe DiMaggio," an African-American player said to Omar. "Where's Marilyn Monroe?" A couple players laughed.

"What's he talking about?" Omar asked Kevin.

"DiMaggio was married to Marilyn Monroe," Kevin replied.

"Really?" Omar said. "The movie star?"

"Yeah, yeah," Kevin said.

When we finished dressing, Manager Maxwell waved us to his office.

"Time to pick a winner," Derek Jeter shouted to us.

That's when we knew the secret was out of the bag.

"Take me out of the lineup!" pleaded a player. "I need a day off!"

About half the team erupted in laughter. I couldn't tell if it was good-natured ribbing or hostile sarcasm. Just know that when the New York Yankees are laughing at you, it's not a good feeling. As we slunk into Mr. Maxwell's office, he could see the worry on our faces.

"Yeah, they all know," he told us as he shut the door. "But don't blame me. I'm just another clown in this circus."

He obviously didn't like working for the Boss.

"But you still got to keep your mouths shut," he ordered, "because the media doesn't know, and it's got to stay that way."

"Okay," I weakly responded.

"Now do your thing," Mr. Maxwell said.

He handed us the lineup card.

"What's really ticking me off," he muttered, "is that I'm now *required* to submit my lineup to Ruffenheimer at 5:30 and then get him your revised lineup by 6:15. It's his way of making sure you're running the show."

Mr. Maxwell left the office, shutting the door hard behind him. I felt an awful numbing sensation go through me. Kevin slumped onto a chair and looked like he was about to cry. Omar was the only one of us who seemed unfazed.

"All right, let's do this," he said as he grabbed the lineup card.

Kevin couldn't get up from his chair, saying he was nauseous. So the Big O and I sat at Mr. Maxwell's computer and started our analysis. Note that this was a lot harder since we were dealing with the Detroit Tigers. We knew the Indians because we were Indians fans. We didn't know the Tigers.

Anyway, Omar and I decided to make just a minor change. Instead of pulling someone out of the lineup, we just moved outfielder Ferdie Gonzalez from the No. 8 spot in the order to No. 5. He was the only player in the lineup with a career average higher than .260 against the Tigers' pitcher. In fact, he had batted .339 with four homers in eleven games against him.

The three of us walked out of the office with our heads down. I handed the card to Mr. Maxwell, who grumbled a "thanks" and walked away.

The players shot us a few glances but left us alone as they chatted among themselves. We all went to the bathroom (with Kevin using the stall) before grabbing the bench in the corner of the dugout.

"I hope Ferdie wears the golden sombrero," Kevin said of Gonzalez.

In baseball lingo, that means he would strike out four times.

We huddled glumly in our corner of the dugout until the game was about to begin. That's when Aurelio Sanchez came by to talk to us.

"It's a ballgame," Sanchez said with a smile, "not a funeral."

We tried to muster our own smiles. Sanchez sat next to us.

"Hey, most of us are cool with you guys," he told us. "It's pretty crazy what the Boss has you doing, but that's him, not you. Plus, you helped us win all three of those games!"

I smiled and nodded.

"I just hope he's paying you," Sanchez said.

"He is," I said.

"Since Sunday, five thousand each for every win," Omar said.

"Ha!" Sanchez exclaimed. "That's hilarious. You put that money toward school, okay? Go to college and get an education. Then someday come back and buy the Yankees."

Kevin smiled and laughed—for the first time in days.

"I'd rather work for you guys than the Boss!" Sanchez said.

Sanchez slapped us five and then walked way. In less than a minute, he had turned our moods around.

This was our first night game as batboys, and there was something exhilarating about running onto the field under the glare of the lights.

I'll never forget seeing Tigers superstar Miguel Cabrera launch a rocket off the left-field fence for a double, and witnessing Alex Avila's towering home run into the night sky. But my biggest thrill of all was retrieving Derek Jeter's bat after the ageless wonder smoked a triple into right-center field. I gripped the sticky handle of Jeter's black beauty and trotted off the diamond as the massive crowd roared for their favorite hero.

As for Ferdie Gonzalez, he went 2-for-5, stroking singles in his first and fifth at-bats. More importantly, he knocked in two runs, helping the Yankees roll to a 6–4 win.

After the game, Omar pointed out that if Gonzalez had batted eighth in the lineup, he would have only batted four times.

"*And,*" Omar said, "he wouldn't have knocked in any runs because the batters ahead of him never reached past first base."

So we were the heroes once again. "Way to go, little dudes!" Gonzalez exclaimed in the locker room, and several players gave us high-fives and fist bumps.

Our dads were ecstatic when they picked us up. "Another five Gs for the Kevin Kernacki college fund!" effused Kevin's dad.

The next day, we were back in Barney Maxwell's office for our five o'clock lineup edit. This game would be a challenge.

"If you can find a way to beat Verlander," said a more-jovial Maxwell, "I'll give you keys to the executive men's room."

The Yankees were about to face Justin Verlander, one of the greatest pitchers of the twenty-first century. As we analyzed Maxwell's lineup, we noticed that Bobby Banks—the Yankees' superstar third baseman—was batting fifth. Banks had been especially horrible against Verlander in his career, going 1-for-31 with seventeen strikeouts.

"He's gotta go," Omar told Kevin and me.

"What do you mean 'go'?" I asked. "You can't take Bobby Banks out of the lineup."

"Hey, we're paid to make the big decisions," Omar said. "We've got to sit him down. His average against Verlander is .032!"

Perhaps we had become too big for our britches, but we stuck with the plan. We crossed out Banks, put our friend Aurelio Sanchez at third, and handed the lineup to Mr. Maxwell. After we explained our reasoning, the manager gave the lineup card a serious pondering.

"Let me discuss this directly with the Boss," he said.

When the game began, Sanchez ran out to third base while Bobby Banks sat quietly on the bench—thankfully, far from us. Again, we were geniuses. Sanchez went 1-for-4—an RBI single— in New York's 2–1 win. Perhaps more importantly, he saved two runs with a diving catch of a Cabrera liner when the bases were loaded.

We were pretty full of ourselves in the locker room after the game, as at least a dozen Yankees players showered us with praise.

"Our three good-luck charms!" Austin Parker said.

All was hunky-dory until a young, muscular guy approached us. I'd seen him once or twice in the locker room before. He had a well-quaffed "chinstrap" beard with short-cropped black hair.

"Hey, can I see you guys for a minute?" he said with a friendly voice.

"Sure," I said, and we followed him into the exercise room, which was unoccupied. The guy closed the door.

And then he locked it.

At that moment, I knew something was about to go terribly wrong.

Chapter 4

BENCHING BOBBY BANKS

Considering that Mr. Muscles had just locked us into the equipment room with him, Omar was pretty cavalier.

"So what's your name—what do you do?" the Big O asked.

The guy picked up a thirty-pound dumbbell and started doing curls.

"People call me Bobby's Boy," the guy said in a New York accent. "I take care of all of Bobby Banks's personal business."

"Ah," Omar said. "I see."

"Oh, yeah?" said Bobby's Boy. "Do you see this?"

In a violent twirl, the guy spun and fired the dumbbell across the room, smashing it loudly against a weight bench. I stepped back, shuddering in fear. Bobby's Boy walked up to us, shoving his finger in our faces.

"If you *ev*-ah," he warned sternly, "take Bobby Banks outta da lineup again, I'll bash your heads against da wall. Do you hear me?"

Scared to death, we each managed to nod. Bobby's Boy stared into Kevin's frightened eyes.

"What did I just say?" Bobby's Boy barked.

"Not . . . to take . . . Bobby out of the lineup," Kevin squeaked, a bead of sweat rolling down his nose.

"That's right," he said. "And if you punks ever tell *anyone* about what just happened here—including your old mans—I'll break all fifteen of your fingers. Got me?"

Again we nodded. He left the room, closing the door behind him. I for one was trembling in my cleats.

"What does he mean, fifteen fingers?" Omar asked. "Does he mean five each? Because we have thirty..."

"He's a moron!" Kevin blurted. "He can't count—that's why he busts heads as Bobby Banks's personal goon!"

"Well, what do we do now?" I asked.

"Nothing," Kevin said. "Just keep our mouths shut and make sure Omar doesn't take Banks out of the lineup again."

"Hey, it's not my fault he was batting .032," Omar said.

After changing out of our uniforms, we met our dads in the Yankees' parking lot. Another $15,000 richer, they greeted us with cheers and hugs—then took us to John & Joe's for "the best pizza in the Bronx."

"You can get any two toppings you'd like," Mr. Ovozi said to Omar, as if he were *really* being generous. "Any two!"

We spent the next day, Wednesday, chilling in the hotel. I ate breakfast in the hotel lobby. Talked to my mom on the phone. Watched a little ESPN News. Took a dip in the pool. Then at four o'clock, it was back to Yankee Stadium.

"So if the Yankees lose tonight," Kevin asked his dad during the limo ride, "we're allowed to go home, right?"

"That's what the Boss said," Mr. Kernacki replied. "But we want to keep that money rolling in, right Kev?"

"That's right," Mr. Ovozi answered.

"And if we win tonight," my dad added, "it's off to Fenway Park for a weekend series. That would really be something."

When we got to the Yankees' locker room, everything seemed normal. Bobby Banks gave us a cold stare, but that was to be expected. Interesting guy, that Bobby Banks. He had played in five All-Star Games with Toronto, hit forty home runs in 2005, and was voted Ontario's "most eligible bachelor"—due to his chiseled good looks.

When the Yankees acquired him a couple years earlier, he was expected to "own" New York. But his skills began to fade, and he was batting just .247 on the day we benched him. I think he was scared that his career was nearing an end.

At five o'clock, we entered Mr. Maxwell's office for our daily lineup change. He was in an especially good mood. After all, his Yankees had won five straight games—thanks to us.

"Do your thing again, boys," he said as he handed us the lineup card. "If we beat Detroit tonight, we're back to .500—and maybe the press will finally get off my back."

Alone in the room, the three of us scoured the lineup and searched Baseball-Reference.com.

"I'm not taking anyone out of the lineup," Kevin said. "I don't want to be stuck in a men's room stall with Austin's Boy or Derek's Boy banging my head on the toilet."

We decided to move speedster Felix Cabellano up in the order, from seventh to first. Detroit's pitcher, Gavin Perry, was a right-hander with a slow delivery. Opponents had stolen seventeen bases in eighteen attempts off him on the year. Cabellano could steal easily whenever he got on base. And batting leadoff in front of New York's finest hitters, he might end up scoring a couple runs.

The wait from 5:30 to game time, 7:05, always felt like an eternity. We continued to sit in the far-left corner of the dugout, hoping that no one would bother us. But at 6:15, our hopes were dashed.

A grizzled reporter, balding with a bushy mustache, walked through the dugout, heading straight for us. He held a tape recorder, a notebook, and a pen. He was onto us.

"Hey," he said. "Andy Plotschman from *The Post*."

I knew that paper. The *New York Post*, like the *Daily News*, was one of New York's infamous "tabloids." They loved to take scandalous stories and splash them on the front page, with a big photo and a huge, sensational headline.

I could see the paper now: "Kids in Charge! Preteen Geeks Boss the Bronx Bombers!"

"What are your names?" Plotschman asked, sticking his recorder in my face.

"I'm not sure we're supposed to talk to you," Omar said.

Mr. Maxwell, talking to a coach near second base, noticed the reporter and began running toward the dugout. I wouldn't have fathomed that the old guy could move that fast. Plotschman realized he had to be quick.

"I heard you guys are making changes to the lineups," he said. "What's going on?"

"Hey!" Maxwell shouted. "Get out of there!"

"Okay," Plotschman responded. "I was just asking—"

Maxwell arrived at the steps, huffing and puffing.

"No reporters in the dugout after six!" he barked. "You know the rules!"

"All right, all right," Plotschman said, and he walked to the tunnel.

"What did you tell him?" Maxwell asked us.

"Nothing, sir," I said. "We didn't even tell him our names."

Maxwell trotted toward the tunnel, probably to have another word with the reporter—or reporters. Kevin buried his face in his hands.

"If he knows, then *everybody* is gonna know," Kev said. "Gosh dang it!"

A few minutes later, Maxwell returned to the dugout and approached us.

"I think I convinced him to keep a lid on it," Maxwell said. "But keep your mouths *shut*. You hear me!"

"Yes, sir," we said.

We fretted on the bench, but after a while, everything seemed to be back to normal.

Until the third inning.

When all heck broke loose.

It all started in the bottom of that inning, with the Tigers up 4–0. Maxwell plopped on the bench with a huff. He turned to us.

"Got any ideas?" he asked, half seriously.

"Actually," Omar said, "I think you should start running. You can steal all day on this pitcher."

Kevin grimaced and whacked Omar's arm. "Shut . . . up!" Kevin scolded.

Maxwell mused over Omar's suggestion.

"Get me the stealing stats on Perry," Maxwell said to one of his coaches.

"Seventeen out of eighteen," Omar said.

Right then, Bobby Banks—who was batting eighth in the lineup—cracked a single up the middle. After the next batter struck out, Cabellano walked, putting runners on first and second. The crowd began to buzz as Derek Jeter strode to the plate. But he flew out to shallow center, prompting me to run out to retrieve DJ's bat.

That was when our world came tumbling down.

As I trotted back to the dugout, a tall teenage boy in the second row stood up, wide-eyed. He stared at his smartphone . . . he stared at me . . . and then he turned to his buddy with a big grin on his face.

"That's him!" he said, pointing right at me.

Before I reached the steps, I stopped and panned the crowd. I felt numb, as if experiencing an out-of-body experience. It all seemed to happen in slow motion. An Asian girl in a Yankees cap mouthed the words *Oh my God!* as she flashed her eyes from her smartphone to me.

I stumbled down the steps in a panic.

"Kevin, where's your phone, where's your phone!" I blubbered.

"What?" he said, looking worried.

"Just . . . get it," I said.

Kevin pulled his smartphone out of his uniform pants. At the same time, I could see Mr. Maxwell flashing signs to the third base coach.

"Google your name," I told Kevin.

"Google my name?" he replied.

"Just do it!" I ordered.

He typed in "Kevin Kernacki," and sure enough, it popped up in an ESPN story, dated "6 minutes ago." Kevin's eyes grew wide, his mouth dropped open.

"Read it," I said.

"Sources have confirmed," Kevin began with a gulp, "that three Yankees batboys—all eleven-year-old students from an unknown suburb of Cleveland—have been making daily changes to the Yankees' lineup for the last six games, including tonight's tilt against the Detroit Tigers. . . ."

At that point, Banks and Cabellano took off on steal attempts.

"It appears," Kevin continued, "that Yankees owner George Ruffenheimer considers the boys his 'lucky charms' after they made suggestions . . ."

Kevin stopped due to the sudden commotion on the diamond. Bobby Banks was grabbing his knee and writhing in pain after being tagged out at third base.

"Oh, no!" cried a player sitting next to us.

I looked over and saw Bobby's Boy on the other end of our dugout, standing on the steps.

"Who called for that steal?" an angry Banks shouted from the field.

Several players, who must have overheard Omar's "steal" suggestion to Maxwell, turned and looked at us. That caught the attention of Bobby's Boy, who stared at us with utter contempt.

"Look," I said to Kevin and Omar, pointing out Bobby's Boy's face of fury.

"We gotta get out of here," Omar said.

"Like *now*," Kevin added.

As nonchalantly as possible, we walked toward the tunnel in the center of the dugout. From the other end, Bobby's Boy did the same.

"Keep it cool," Omar said as we entered the tunnel. "There's a security guard up ahead."

Bobby's Boy also walked at a casual pace, but he was surely stalking us. The words that he had uttered the day before rang between my ears. *"I'll bash your heads against da wall."*

"He's gonna kill us," Kevin whispered. "I just know it."

We entered the clubhouse, and so did Bobby's Boy. With several people milling around, our stalker remained in control. But when I turned around, I could see the rage in his eyes.

I'm not sure why, but we were drawn to the door that led to the parking lot. Maybe, we thought, if we left Yankee Stadium, we would wake up from this nightmare.

Still in our Yankee uniforms, spikes and all, we approached the exit door. I turned the handle and pushed the door open. And then we ran.

Chapter 5

RUNNING SCARED IN NEW YORK

What a sight we were: a trio of batboys, in our Yankee pinstripes, running like former Yankee Mickey "Mick the Quick" Rivers down River Avenue, alongside Yankee Stadium.

Bobby's Boy was on our tail, trotting fast but not too fast. He still didn't want to look conspicuous. He wouldn't assault us on the streets—not with hundreds of people milling around the ballpark.

Or would he? I turned around and saw a maniacal look of vengeance in his eyes. His livelihood depended on Bobby Banks's best interests. Now the aging Banks had suffered a knee injury—perhaps a career-ender. And in this goon's mind, it was all our fault.

"What's he planning on doing?" huffed Omar as we scurried down the sidewalk.

"It's the Bronx," Kevin replied. "He's probably gonna corner us in an alley and break our kneecaps ... or whack us."

With the pre-dusk sun shining like a golden spotlight, we had no place to hide. As Bobby's Boy continued his pursuit—at about thirty yards back—everyone was gawking at us.

"It's da Yankee batboys!" cried one guy. "Dey're on da loose!"

My mom always said that women can't run in heels. I'm sure that's true, but running in spikes on cement was no picnic either. We were running out of breath.

"Let's go in here," Omar said, and we followed him into the Hard Rock Cafe. The place was packed with Yankee fans watching the game, which was now 4–1 Tigers. Slithering past the hostess, we tried to lose ourselves in the crowd.

"Look at that!" Omar said, pointing to one of the displays. "That electric guitar, it's white with Yankee pinstripes."

"Yeah, and so is my outfit!" Kevin retorted. "We've got to get out of these clothes."

"What are we supposed to do?" I said. "Run around New York in baseball cleats and our underwear?"

A big, jowly man overheard me. "You wouldn't be the first!" he quipped, and then doubled over in a belly laugh.

Kevin tried to call his dad, but he couldn't get a dial tone.

"Crap," he said.

"Look," Omar said, pointing to a TV on the wall.

"Breaking News," read the ESPN ticker. "Sources have confirmed that three Yankee batboys..."

It was the same story that had gone viral twenty minutes ago. Again, people pointed and stared. But our bigger concern was Bobby's Boy, who entered the restaurant and beelined toward us.

"Let's get outta here," I said.

As our nemesis pursued us, we zigzagged around tables and back out the front door.

We ran as fast as we could down River Avenue, but Bobby's Boy left Hard Rock, too—and now sprinted after us.

"Let's go in there," Omar said, pointing to a place called Billy's.

"We can't," I said. "It's a bar."

"Then the next place," he said.

The place next door was called Yankee Bar & Grill.

"That's a bar, too," Kevin huffed.

"What about the—," Omar began. But right next to Yankee Bar & Grill was Stan's Sports Bar.

"Dang it!" Kevin cried. "Do ya gotta be drunk off your rocker to be a Yankees fan?"

We tried to lose Bobby's Boy by ducking through an alley—in retrospect, a dangerous move that could have led to our demise. We did emerge on another street and found ourselves in front of . . . Yankee Tavern, "The Original Sports Bar."

"Aargh!" Kevin crowed.

"Let's just go in," I said. But as I grabbed the door handle, Bobby's Boy emerged from around the corner and took a swipe at Kevin from behind.

"Ahhhhh!" Kevin screamed.

Anyone who has ever seen Kevin play shortstop knows that he's got lightning-fast reflexes. He eluded the predator's grasp and bolted down the sidewalk like a bunny with its tail on fire. We followed. Bobby's Boy, who was scowled at by an old lady, tried to play it cool. But soon, he was off to the races again.

We ran to nearby E. 161st Street and headed for the subway. Thankfully, I had a $20 bill in my pocket, but the ticket line was long. Soon, Bobby's Boy was waiting a few people behind us, which made me very edgy.

A little kid, holding his dad's hand in one hand and a Yankees yearbook in the other, waited in front of us. He stared back in awe.

"Are you real Yankee batboys?" he asked.

"Yeah, kind of," I said.

"Can I have your autographs?" he asked.

Oh, the price of fame! Omar and I quickly signed our names on the yearbook. Kevin, the kid hater, scribbled "Reggie Jackson."

We soon got our tickets, spun through the turnstiles, and ran to the farthest train car.

Still stuck at the turnstile, Bobby's Boy couldn't have possibly seen which train car we had entered, especially since we slunk down in our seats, below the windows.

"Is your phone working?" Omar asked Kevin.

"No," he replied with a grimace as he pounded various buttons. "I don't know what's going on."

"Well, we'll get off at the next stop and call my dad from there," I said, thinking we would just borrow a phone.

"At least Bobby's Boy is off our tail," Omar said.

"Yeah," Kevin said, his face dripping with sweat. "It's time to get out of this stinkin' city."

At the next stop, we left the subway and headed up the steps to the loud, dirty street. It was dark now, and streetlights and headlights illuminated the night. We walked barely ten feet until, on the corner, we saw him. Bobby's Boy. Staring right at us.

"Why ride the subway," he shouted at us through the din of the traffic, "when you can take a taxi cab."

Once again, I thought, it was time to run. But by the look on Kevin's face, I realized we weren't going anywhere. With eyes burning and steam practically coming out of his ears, Kevin marched straight up to Bobby's Boy. A group of Latino teens, a half dozen of them, curtailed their street-corner powwow at the sight of this strange confrontation.

"If you want to bash my head in," Kevin screamed at Bobby's Boy, wagging his finger like a manager at an umpire, "then just go ahead and do it! Put me out of my misery!"

"We came to this stupid city a week ago," Kev continued, "because a spoiled little *fat* kid saw us on TV, and the next thing we know we're being held captive by some nutso owner who forces us to make changes that cause *our* team to lose and makes psycho players send thugs like you out to murder us!"

Spit was flying out of Kevin's mouth. We all stood by, dumbfounded.

"*Bash* our heads in!" Kevin told Bobby's Boy. "Go ahead! Have a field day! You'll make every front-page tabloid headline in New York City: 'Banks's Boy Kills Batboy Stooges!' Just remember this: it wasn't *our* fault we took your boy out of the lineup! He was batting a freakin' .033!"

"Oh-32," Omar corrected.

"Oh-32!" Kevin blared. "He stinks! He's washed up! Go find another overpriced prima donna who needs a goon for hire!"

Kevin walked right up to Bobby's Boy, looked up at his face, and tapped his own chin.

"Now are you gonna hit me, or are you gonna hit me?" Kevin blared. "'Cause I'm ready!"

As Bobby's Boy looked down at his courageous little nemesis, he had no idea how to respond. He ended up just waving his hand in front of Kev's face.

"Ah, forget it," Bobby's Boy said, and he walked away.

"Yeahhhhhh!" screamed the Latino boys from the sideline. They beamed their approval and pumped their fists, going "woo, woo, woo!"

Omar and I went to congratulate the hero. Kevin looked down at his hands, which were shaking uncontrollably. The poor kid. He was an emotional wreck.

But before he could even speak, Omar put his arm around Kev's shoulder.

"Come on, buddy," Omar said as he led Kevin down the New York street. "It's time to go home."

We walked down the block and stopped at Dino's Italian Kitchen, where they allowed us to use the phone to call our dads.

As we waited to get picked up, the owner, Dino, gave us a large Dino Supreme—sausage, black olives, green peppers, onions, and mushrooms. Dino was a Yankees fan. That was the least he could do, he said, for helping his team win six straight games.

That's right, the Yankees came back to win that game, 5–4, and Banks's injury wasn't serious at all—just a sprain. We heard all about it on TV at the airport.

We expected to deal with some questions from the Cleveland media when we got home, but that would be nothing compared to the pressures we dealt with in New York.

"Besides," Mr. Kernacki said, "you made our Indians lose three games, but the first-place Tigers lost three. So we didn't lose any ground."

"And," Mr. Ovozi said, "you each gained $20,000 for your college fund!"

"Where do you want to go to college, Kev?" my dad asked.

I knew what was coming.

"Anywhere in America," Kevin replied. "Except New York."

Read each title in The Baseball Geeks Adventures

A HALL Lot of Trouble at Cooperstown
The Baseball Geeks Adventures Book 1

When Joe, Kevin, and Omar take a trip to Cooperstown to save Kevin's dad, will the boys be able save themselves from the "trouble" they get into?

ISBN: 978-1-62285-118-8

Foul Ball Frame-up at Wrigley Field
The Baseball Geeks Adventures Book 2

After Omar is "framed" for an incident that was out of his hands, can Joe and Kevin save their friend from becoming one of the biggest curses in history?

ISBN: 978-1-62285-123-2

The Treasure Hunt Stunt at Fenway Park
The Baseball Geeks Adventures Book 3

Joe, Kevin, and Omar want a shot at the Treasure Hunt Round. But can the Geeks beat the Little League Champs before they "stunt" the Geeks' chances of winning it all?

ISBN: 978-1-62285-128-7

Bossing the Bronx Bombers at Yankee Stadium
The Baseball Geeks Adventures Book 4

When the Geeks are invited to watch a game from a luxury suite, Joe, Kevin, and Omar find themselves in a bad situation when they start making some "bossy" calls.

ISBN: 978-1-62285-133-1